OSCAR'S DAY OUT

Palmetto Publishing Group
Charleston, SC

Oscar's Day Out: An Urban Tail
Copyright © 2018 by Gina Zadrozny
All rights reserved

Photos by Mike McCawley
First Edition

Printed in the United States

ISBN-13: 978-1-64111-227-7
ISBN-10: 1-64111-227-1

OSCAR'S DAY OUT

AN URBAN TAIL

Gina M. Zadrozny

DEDICATION

To all of the students I have had or will have, for allowing me to read to you. Thank you for being a captive audience to my favorite part of the day, Read Aloud. The time we spend together reading my favorite stories, that in turn, become your favorite stories, is the very best part of being a teacher.

HI! I'M OSCAR.

I am a six-year-old dog, and I live in a big city called Chicago. A lot of people ask what *kind* of dog I am, and my mom always tells them the same thing: I'm a little bit of everything. But according to my DNA test, I am part bull mastiff and part Boston terrier. I don't really know what that means exactly; I just know I am very SCRUFFY! People are always shocked to hear what type of dog I am, but I don't really understand why. I am exactly the kind of dog I am supposed to be.

I was born on the streets. I didn't have a home at first. Somehow, I found my way to a shelter, and that's where my mom found me. She always tells me the story of how she went to the shelter to see about another dog named Mickey, but he turned out to be a little too small. She was ready to leave without a dog when she saw me! I was in a different room with a different lady who thought I was too big. Would you believe it—that lady left with Mickey, and well, you guessed it, my mom got me!

My name was P.J., but my mom renamed me . . . Oscar. I remember it was really cold out when I went home. I didn't even want to leave the warm house to go potty. I was sort of worried that I wouldn't be let back in! I never had a home before but knew that it was pretty great and I wanted to be in it as much as possible. Eventually, I started to realize that even after I went outside, I always got to go back inside . . . home.

My mom is pretty great—she thinks she rescued me, but I think we rescued each other. She's my very best human friend. She's always gentle; she kisses me goodnight and says, "Sweet dreams." She always lets me take my time smelling everything too, and that's important to me. I have best dog friends too, but I will introduce you to them another time.

I really want to tell you about a special day when I got to go to all the places my mom went. Most of the time, dogs have to be alone when our owners go out, so it's always nice to be able to go with my mom when I can. She always tries to find places that don't mind me visiting: restaurants, parks, even some stores! I really love my neighborhood—the smells, the sights, the people. I know so many of my neighbors; some have four legs, and some have two!

Coffee is always our first stop. It was nice out, so we sat outside so my mom could read for a while. I really like when we do this because I get to lie down on the sidewalk and wait for people to come and pet me. Sometimes, if I am really good, my mom gets me a "puppacino," which is really just a fancy name for whipped cream in a cup. Boy, is it yummy!

There's even a coffee shop by my house that lets me inside. I love it there because the owner gives me bacon. It is probably the best thing I get to eat, and when we're anywhere near there, I try to pull my mom in that direction so we can go in.

After coffee, my mom had to stop in to a place to get money—I think it's called a bank. They have a BIG jar of bones on the counter, so I sat nicely and got one. I love when we go there too!

There's also a little place that has a lot of aisles and shelves. There are so many things to look at and smell: paint cans, tools, cleaning stuff. Sometimes my mom has to buy something, but today, she just took me in there so the really nice people could pet me, they all love dogs! They gave me a treat too!

We also went to the farmer's market in the town square today. They always have fresh flowers, and I tried to lift my leg on them, but my mom caught me just before I did!

Our neighborhood is really friendly, and it always seems like my mom stops to talk to people on our walks. Sometimes I get tired and lie down. Every once in a while, someone will ask her if I am all right but she tells them that I am just really lazy. I don't know what lazy is exactly, but I do know I like to sleep a lot.

Even though I love to spend the day with my mom, out running errands, I can't wait to get back home to my cozy bed.

Well, that's just a little bit about me: a scruffy dog that was born on the street. A dog that looks like a lot of different things. A happy dog with a great mom and a lot of great neighbors. I sure hope that little dog Mickey is as happy as I am!

THE END